STERLING CHILDREN'S BOOKS
New York

An Imprint of Sterling Publishing Co., Inc.
1166 Avenue of the Americas
New York, NY 10036

Text © 2017 by Phillis Gershator
Illustrations © 2017 by David Walker

ISBN 978-1-4549-1981-0

Distributed in Canada by Sterling Publishing
c/o Canadian Manda Group, 664 Annette Street
Toronto, Ontario, Canada M6S 2C8.
Distributed in the United Kingdom by GMC Distribution Services
Castle Place, 166 High Street, Lewes, East Sussex, England BN7 1XU
Distributed in Australia by NewSouth Books
45 Beach Street, Coogee, NSW 2034, Australia

For information about custom editions, special sales, and premium and corporate purchases,
please contact Sterling Special Sales at 800-805-5489 or specialsales@sterlingpublishing.com.

Manufactured in China
Lot #:
2   4   6   8   10   9   7   5   3   1
12/16

www.sterlingpublishing.com

The artwork for this book was prepared using pencil and acrylic paints.

TIME
for a
NAP

by Phillis Gershator
illustrated by David Walker

STERLING CHILDREN'S BOOKS
New York

From Monday to Sunday
how busy we'll be.

We've got places to go
and people to see!

Monday we shop.
What do we need?

Carrots, cabbage,
books to read.

Monday

shop

Try on shoes,

choose a cap—

What time is it?

Time for a nap!

No frowns, no fuss,
no *boo hoo hoos.*

Buckle up for
a snoozy snooze.

Tuesday morning

Tuesday
playground

hop, skip, jump.

Ride the seesaw,

bump a rump.

Too tired to hop.
No zip, no zap—

What time is it?

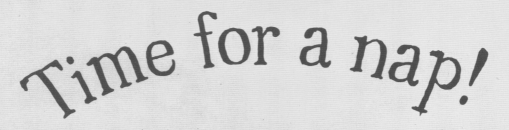

Time for a nap!

At home we pick
our favorite spot.
A rug, a mat,
a bed, a cot.

Wednesday

story time

Wednesday morning
story time.
Join a circle,
make a rhyme.

Sing a song,
clappity-clap—

What time is it?

Time for a nap!

Can't catch me!
I like to play.

I don't *want*
to nap today.

Thursday, Friday
we work hard.

Do the laundry,
weed the yard.

Thursday
Laundry

Friday
Yard
work

Sweep up every
little scrap.

What time is it?

Time for a nap!

Nobody's tired.
Nobody's cranky.
Bring my bunny!
Bring my blankie!

Saturday, Sunday
we relax.

Doodle, dawdle,
nibble snacks.

Sing and dance,
Tappity-tap.

What time is it?

Time for a nap!

And nap time kisses on each cheek, every day of every week.

When we wake up,
our nap is done.

What time is it?

IT'S TIME FOR FUN!